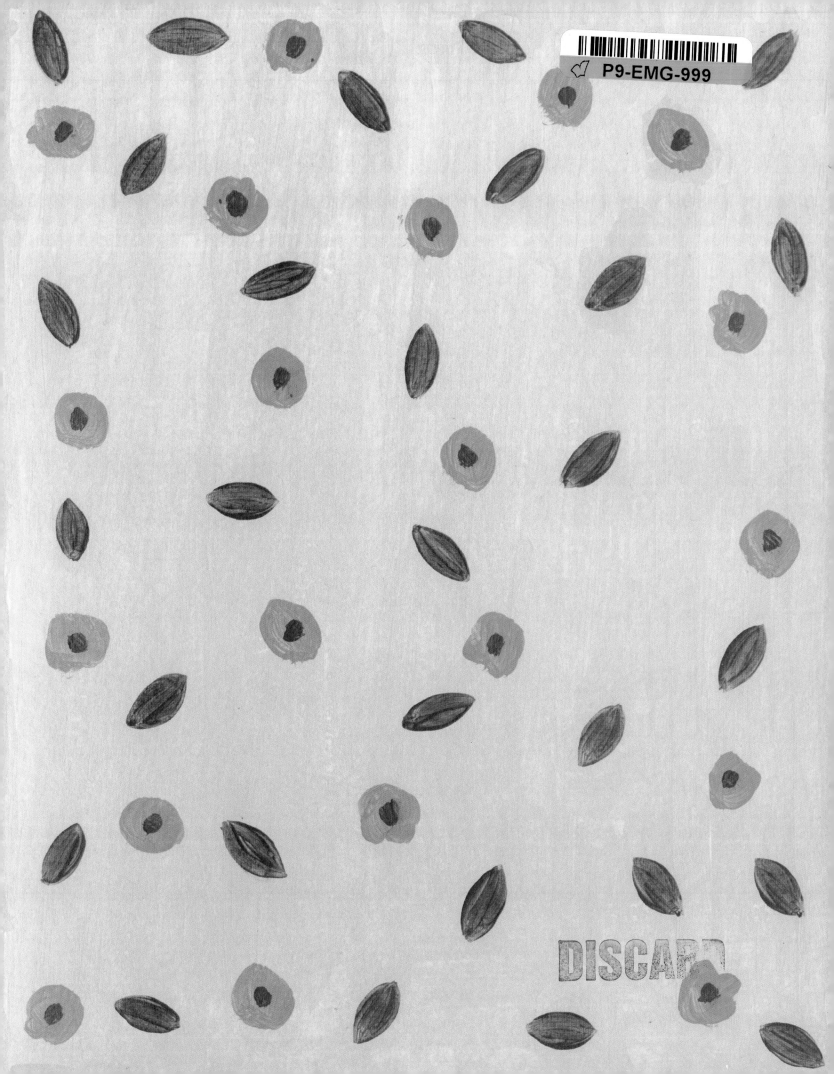

*For my
brothers,
Ronnie and
Michael
—K. D.*

*To my
high school
art teacher,
Ms. Kim
—C. R.*

ATHENEUM BOOKS FOR YOUNG READERS
An imprint of Simon & Schuster Children's Publishing Division
1230 Avenue of the Americas, New York, New York 10020
Text copyright © 2014 by Kelly DiPucchio
Illustrations copyright © 2014 by Christian Robinson
All rights reserved, including the right of reproduction in whole or in
part in any form.
ATHENEUM BOOKS FOR YOUNG READERS is a registered
trademark of Simon & Schuster, Inc.
Atheneum logo is a trademark of Simon & Schuster, Inc.
For information about special discounts for bulk purchases, please
contact Simon & Schuster Special Sales at 1-866-506-1949 or
business@simonandschuster.com.
The Simon & Schuster Speakers Bureau can bring authors to your live
event. For more information or to book an event, contact the Simon &
Schuster Speakers Bureau at 1-866-248-3049 or visit our website at
www.simonspeakers.com.
Interior design by Ann Bobco. Jacket design by Christian Robinson and
Ann Bobco.

The text for this book is set in Adobe Caslon Pro.
The illustrations for this book are rendered in acrylic paint.
Manufactured in the United States of America
0714 PCR
10 9 8 7 6 5 4 3
Library of Congress Cataloging-in-Publication Data
DiPucchio, Kelly S.
Gaston / Kelly DiPucchio ; illustrated by Christian Robinson. — 1st ed.
p. cm.
Summary: A proper bulldog raised in a poodle family and a tough
poodle raised in a bulldog family meet one day in the park.
ISBN 978-1-4424-5102-5 (hardcover)
ISBN 978-1-4424-5103-2 (eBook)
[1. Poodles—Fiction. 2. Bulldog—Fiction. 3. Dogs—Fiction.
4. Individuality—Fiction.] I. Robinson, Christian, ill. II. Title.
PZ7.D6219Gas 2014
[E]—dc23   2012031987

Gaston

WORDS BY **KELLY DiPUCCHIO**

PICTURES BY **CHRISTIAN ROBINSON**

 Atheneum Books for Young Readers   New York · London · Toronto · Sydney · New Delhi

atheneum

Mrs. Poodle admired her new puppies.

Fi-Fi, Foo-Foo, Ooh-La-La, and Gaston.

Would you like  to see them again?

Fi-Fi,

Foo-Foo,

Ooh-La-La,

and *Gaston*.

Perfectly precious, aren't they?

Mrs. Poodle
thought so too.
The puppies grew
(as puppies do).
Three were no bigger
than teacups.

The fourth, however, continued to grow.
And grow. Until he was the size of a *teapot*.

Mrs. Poodle took pride in teaching her puppies how to be proper pooches. They were taught to sip. *Never slobber!*

"Good."

"Well done."

"Very nice."

"Nice try."

They were taught to yip. *Never yap!*

And they were taught to walk with grace. *Never race!*

Tip.   **Toe.**   **Tippy-toe.**

WHOA!

The puppies were also taught
how to look pretty in pink,
nibble their kibble,
and ride in style.

Whatever the lesson, **Gaston**
always worked the hardest,
practiced the longest,
and smiled the biggest.

Mrs. Poodle was very pleased
with all her puppies,

Foo-Foo, *Ooh-La-La*,

Fi-Fi,

and **Gaston**.

Spring arrived, and the proud mother was
eager to show off her darlings. She took them
to the park for their very first stroll in public.

There was much to see. Daffodils. Ducklings. Dogs.

Oh dear.
Who do we have here?

ROCKY,

RICKY,

BRUNO,

and
ANTOINETTE.

Would you like to see them again?

ROCKY,

RICKY,

BRUNO,

and
ANTOINETTE.

This was more than a little awkward.
The mothers sized up the pups.
The pups sized up one another.

"It seems there's been a terrible mistake,"
Mrs. Bulldog said, breaking the silence.

"*Oui, oui,*" Mrs. Poodle agreed sadly. "Whatever shall we do?"
Mrs. Bulldog could not come up with an answer.
"I guess we'll let them decide," she replied at last.

Gaston and **ANTOINETTE** were young, but even they could see that there had been a mix-up. The two puppies began to circle around and around the group.

Gaston walked with grace.
ANTOINETTE raced.
Gaston yipped.
ANTOINETTE yapped.

And when they
finally
came to a stop ...
the puppies
had traded places.

There.
That *looked* right ...

it just didn't *feel* right.

That evening **ANTOINETTE** tried to fit in with her new sisters, but she did not like anything proper or precious or pink.

PHOOEY!

On the other side of town, **Gaston** tried to fit in with his new brothers, but he did not like anything brutish or brawny or brown.

Ick!

ANTOINETTE and *Gaston* weren't the only ones

who were having a hard time adjusting.

The next morning Mrs. Poodle forgot
all about being proper and raced
back to the park.

Mrs. Bulldog was already there
waiting with her burly brood.

"It seems *we've* made a terrible mistake!"
she nearly shouted.

"*Oui, oui!*" Mrs. Poodle agreed happily.

This time **Gaston** and ANTOINETTE
wasted no time trading places.

There.
That looked right.
And it felt right, too.

From that day forward the families met
in the park every afternoon to play.

ROCKY, RICKY, BRUNO, and **ANTOINETTE**
taught the poodle puppies a thing or two about being tough.

Likewise, **Fi-Fi**, **Foo-Foo**, **Ooh-La-La**, and **Gaston** taught the bulldog puppies a thing or two about being tender.

And many years later, when **Gaston** and **ANTOINETTE**
fell in love and had puppies of their own,
they taught them to be whatever they wanted to be.

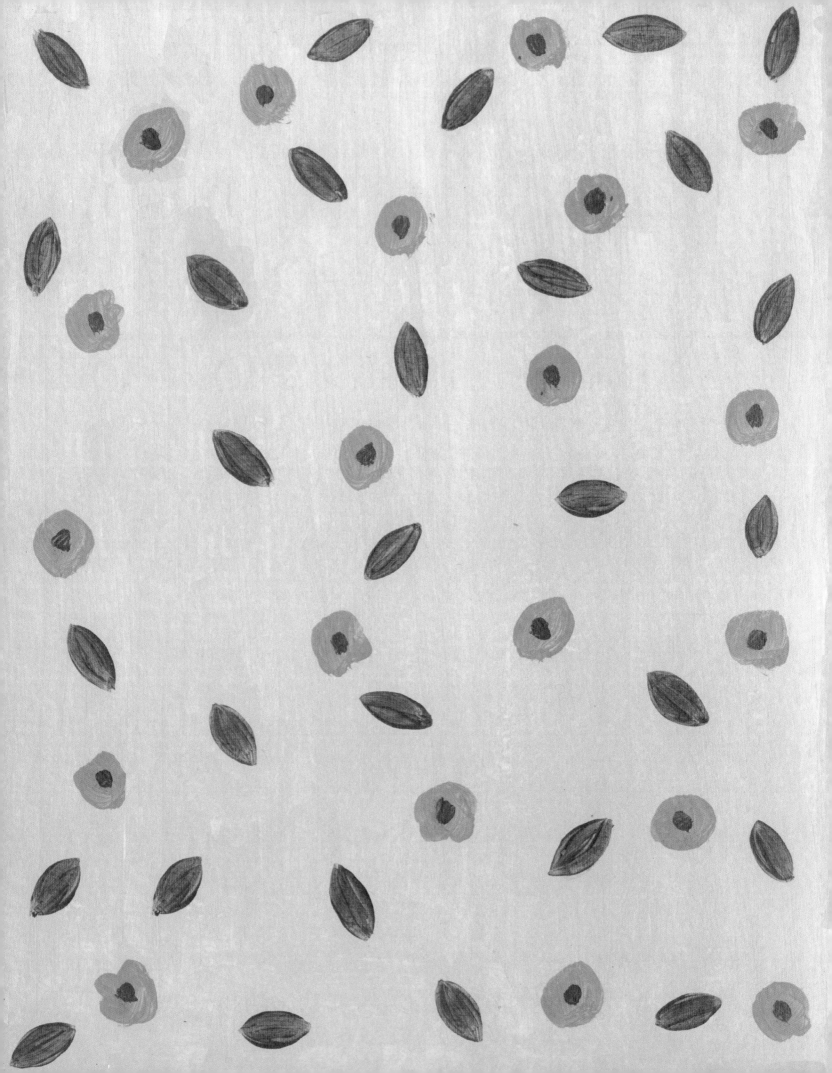